A PAiR OF
JACKS

ORCHARD BOOKS
338 Euston Road, London NW1 3BH
Orchard Books Australia
Level 17/207 Kent Street, Sydney, NSW 2000
First published in hardback in Great Britain in 2009 by Orchard Books
First published in paperback in 2010
ISBN 978 1 84616 751 5 (hardback)
ISBN 978 1 40830 775 5 (paperback)
Text © Michael Lawrence 2009
Illustrations © Tony Ross 2009
The rights of Michael Lawrence to be identified as the author and
of Tony Ross to be identified as the illustrator of this work
have been asserted by them in accordance with the
Copyright, Designs and Patents Act, 1988.
A CIP catalogue record for this book is available from the British Library.
1 3 5 7 9 10 8 6 4 2 (hardback)
1 3 5 7 9 10 8 6 4 2 (paperback)
Printed in Great Britain
Orchard Books is a division of Hachette Children's Books,
an Hachette UK company.
www.hachette.co.uk

JACK and the BROOMSTICK

AND

FROM a JACK TO a KING

MICHAEL LAWRENCE

TONY ROSS

ORCHARD BOOKS

JACK and the BROOMSTICK

Now Jack Withersnitch of Nethersnitch-in-the-Mire wasn't very bright. You have to know this before we go any further. Why? Because if Jack had been bright he wouldn't have brought home the broomstick and I wouldn't have been able to bore the pants off you telling you about it.

Jack and his widowed mother – a nagging old shrew with a moustache on her lip and a boil on her bum – lived in a tumbledown hovel surrounded by a wonky wooden fence. They were as poor as dead church mice, these two, and getting poorer by the minute. This is because they lived by their wits, and there was a wit shortage in Nethersnitch-in-the-Mire.

'If we don't do something soon,'

Mother said,

'we'll end up like the cat.'

'You mean stuffed

and stood on top of the dresser?'

said Jack.

THE CAT

'I remember an old tale,' his mother mused, ignoring him as usual, 'about another young layabout called Jack. *Jack and the Beanstalk* it was called. I think I used to tell it to you at bedtime when you were younger and shorter.'

Jack yawned. 'You must have. I come over all sleepy every time you mention it.'

'This other idle good-for-nothing of a Jack,' Mother went on, 'he set off one day to sell the family cow at the market, and on the way he met a peddler who offered him some beans for the cow.'

'Yes, I remember,' Jack said, yawning himself stupid.

'And when Jack brought the beans home his poor widowed mother was so furious that she threw them out the window. Ah, but in the morning what do you think they found there?'

'A beanstalk,'

said Jack,

curling up on the floor

and shoving his thumb

in his gob.

'A beanstalk,' said his mother. 'Growing up and up and up, it was, all the way to the clouds. And when Jack climbed to the top he found a huuuuuge castle and a giant with a voice like a bad bellyache, who...Jack?

Jack, are you listening to me?'

'Zzzzzzzz,'

snored Jack.

Kicking him affectionately in the ribs, Mother said: 'My son, you must do what that other waste of space did. You must go and get us some beans that will grow into a giant beanstalk overnight, and then you must climb up it into the clouds and steal a giant's hen that lays golden eggs, his golden harp that plays like a dream, and his solid gold chamber pot so we can pee richly ever after.'

'Mother,' Jack said, 'I think it's time you started seeing that therapist again.'

'Up now, Jack!'

Mother commanded.

'To the market road with you!

And don't forget the cow.

You'll need her to exchange for the beans.'

So, with a hefty sigh and the family cow on a bit of old rope, Jack Withersnitch set off. It was a pointless mission, he knew. There was absolutely no chance of meeting a peddler on the market road. That sort of thing only happened in stories.

'Mornin', lad,'

quoth a peddler,

stepping out from behind a tree.

'Curses,' said Jack.

'And where are you a'going with yon cow?' the peddler said, still quothing.

'Mind your own business,' snapped the youth churlishly.

'Off to market, I reckons. Must be, cos the only other thing along this road is the public lavs and they been vandalised.'

'Oh no,' said Jack, crossing his legs.

The peddler set aside the broomstick he'd been carrying over his shoulder and inspected the cow, looking first in one ear, then the udder.

'Fine beast. What'll you take for her?'

'She's not for sale,' Jack said. 'Not unless,' he added with a nervous laugh, 'you happen to have some beans with you.'

'Beans?' the peddler quotheth. 'I'm a broomstick-maker, what would I be doing with beans?'

Jack uncrossed his legs. 'That's a relief,' he said, and wet himself.

'But today's your lucky day, my friend.'

'Not so far it isn't,' said Jack, plucking miserably at his tights.

'Oh but it is. You see,

I have just **one** broomstick left

(sold the rest at market) and this...

this is a **magic** one.'

Jack stopped plucking his tights. 'A magic broomstick?' He dried his fingers on his hair. 'What does it do?'

'Young sir,' the peddler answered, 'magic is a secret thing. Talk about it and it don't work. Now will you swap your cow for my magic broomstick or do I make someone else's day?'

'Well I don't know,' Jack said. 'Mother told me to come back with beans. She didn't say anything about broomsticks.'

'Tell you what I'll do,' the stranger said (or quoth if you prefer). 'I'll give you the magic broomstick for the cow and throw in this silver coin for the bit of old rope round her neck. Money for old rope.

Can't say fairer than that, can I?'

But when Jack returned home and showed his mother what he'd got for the cow and the rope, Mother was not pleased, especially when she bit clear through the coin.

'Must I do everything myself?' she screamed. 'I said beans, Jack, beans not brooms. You can't grow a beanstalk from a broom!'

'But Mother,
it's a magic
broomstick!'

'Foolish boy, that peddlor saw you coming, probably from behind a tree. Oh Jack, Jack, what am I to do with you?'

With this she seized the axe from the hearth and hacked the broom to bits and flung the bits out of the window.

Quailing before his mother's wrath Jack went to bed while it was still light, without his supper. Falling asleep after much tossing and turning and twiddling and twerking, he dreamed of the broomstick he'd exchanged for the cow, and the beans that he hadn't. He felt pretty stupid, even in the dream. When he heard Mother calling him he imagined he was still dreaming.

'Now see what *you* done,

Jack Withersnitch! Look out here!'

But he wasn't dreaming.
It was morning,
and Mother was shrieking
from downstairs.

He fell out of bed with a groan and hopped to tho window in tho only slipper he could find. In the yard below, Mother scowled up at him from a forest of broomsticks that had grown to full height overnight from the scattered sticks of the peddler's broom.

'So it **was magic**,'

he whispered to his astonished self.

'Must have been,'

his astonished self whispered back.

Then witches began to arrive.

In droves they came, on rickety bikes, on witchity pogo-sticks, on broomsticks so old and lumpy they had to sit on cushions.

There were ta**ll** witches
and **short** witches,
thin witches
and fat,

and witches you couldn't **begin** to describe except to say that they were ug**ly**.

Jack gulped and
went downstairs
to sit on a stool
in a dim,
dark,
cobwebby corner
and await a
motherly whack.

But in a while the cackling outside ceased and Mother came in weighed down by an apron full of gold coins.

Real ones.

'We're rich!'
she cried.
'I knew
that broomstick
was a good deal.'

Jack left his stool and went to the door. The witches were gone, the new broomsticks too – all but one, which hadn't found a buyer.

'Mind you,' said Mother, never satisfied, 'we'd be richer still with a beanstalk to the clouds.' She sighed. 'Ah well. A small fortune's better than no fortune at all, I suppose. Now Jack, I want you to go to market and buy food. Lots of it. A whole cartload. With this much gold we'll be able to stock up and live like a queen and her idiot son for months.'

So off to market went Jack Withersnitch with the apron full of gold coins and a cart to bring all the food home in. He had to pull the cart himself as they'd eaten the horse last Tuesday, but he didn't mind, for he had a plan to make his mother really pleased with him.

When he returned, pulling the laden cart, Jack was grinning from lobe to lobe, partly because of what he'd bought at the market, and partly because the public lavs had been fixed and his tights were dry.

'Mother!' he called. 'Come and see what I've got!'

His mother rushed out, eager to view the delicacies her beloved son had brought home. 'Ooh, I can't wait,' she squealed. 'We'll have ourselves a right royal feast tonight and no mis...take...'

She stopped, and rubbed her eyes, hoping they were playing tricks on her.

They weren't.

'Oh Jack,'
she wailed.
'Jack,
what have you done?'

'I did what you wanted the first time,' the youth replied proudly. 'But I didn't need to exchange anything this time. I could buy beans. So I did!'

'You spent all the gold on **these**?' said Mother.

'**Every sparkling bit!**' Jack cried with rosy-cheeked glee.

'Now we can grow a beanstalk to the clouds and nick stuff from the giant who lives up there and be as rich as can be and happy ever after – or at least until the day you die!'

Mother ground her teeth
and spat one out.

'There's beans and there's beans, Jack,
and this kind won't grow into any kind of
beanstalk with a giant on top.'

'Why not?' said Jack, puzzled beyond
his years.

'Because they are baked beans, Jack. Because they are canned beans, Jack. Because you can't grow nothing from canned baked beans, you half-baked bean-brained boy. Worse still, the can-opener hasn't been invented yet, so we can't even eat the bally things.'

She seized the one broomstick she hadn't sold to the witches and whacked him across the shoulders with it.

'I rue the day I ever bore such a useless son!' she screeched. 'Get them cans out of my sight or it'll be early bed without supper for life for you!'

Casting the last broom aside she went indoors and sobbed on the kitchen table till the polish came off, while Jack, sad Jack, dug a pit in the yard for the cartload of cans. As an afterthought he tossed in the last broom before sneaking upstairs to an early bed without any supper.

Next morning Jack woke to an unfamiliar sound; a clanking sort of sound, like bits of metal nudging one another in a gentle breeze. Curious, he got up and hopped to the window in his slipper. The window was unusually dark for daytime. Something was blocking out the light.

He went downstairs. 'Mother?'

She wasn't there. He went outside to look for her. Still no sign, but in the yard, growing tall and straight from yesterday's pit, stood a giant broomstick with a myriad twig-like branches; and on each branch a dozen or more brand-new unlabelled cans of beans hung glinting in the sun.

Jack fell back, astonished, and sought the top of the broomstick. So tall was it that its upper branches, dense with gleaming cans, vanished into the clouds. And way up there, just below the sky, a tiny figure climbed hand over hand over hand.

'MOTHER!' Jack bellowed, and cupped an ear for her reply.

None came.

Either she was too high to hear or she was ignoring him as usual. Catching a final flash of her best blue bloomers merging with the clouds, Jack recalled how often Mother had said that the only way to get a job done properly was to do it herself. Well, now she was doing it herself. Rather than send him after the giant's golden horde and risk him bringing back brass, she was fetching it personally!

Days passed, and Jack Withersnitch inspected the gigantic broomstick every waking hour, constantly expecting a flash of his mother's bloomers coming down. But never did he catch a sight of them, or her. As she wasn't there to nag him, Jack left his bed unmade, the dishes undone, the floors unswept, and avoided all the other boring chores she made him do when she was around. He'd never had such an easy time of it, or such a peaceful one.

But late one morning a mighty clanking outside his darkened window woke Jack with a start. 'Mother!' he cried in panic, jumping out of bed, into his slipper, and hopping downstairs to start the dishes.

But it wasn't Mother.

No. It was a giant who lived in the clouds.

'Save me!' said the giant, bending down and looking in. 'There's this little old baggage up there who keeps telling me to hand over my hen that lays golden eggs, my golden harp that plays like a dream, and my solid gold chamber pot. I tell her I don't possess such things, but she refuses to believe me and whacks my knees.'

'I thought all giants had stuff like that,' said Jack.

'Not this one,' said the giant. 'I'm poor. Can't sell my inventions for love nor money.'

'Inventions? You invent things? What sort of things?'

The giant frowned. 'Are you asking out of politeness or because you really want to know?'

'I really want to know,' answered Jack, who had indeed been asking out of politeness.

'Come out here then, and I'll tell you about them.'

Jack went outside
and sat on the step,
and the giant sat on the
garden shed, one
enormous leg
crossed over
the other.

'My greatest inventions,' the giant said, 'the ones I'm most pleased with, are the alarm clock that goes off underwater, the jug that pours warm beer endlessly, and the wig that lights up in the dark (handy for bald men on starless nights, I thought). Oh, and would you like to see my latest?'

'I can't wait,' said Jack, still being polite.

The giant tugged a peculiarly-shaped silver object from the pocket of his jerkin.

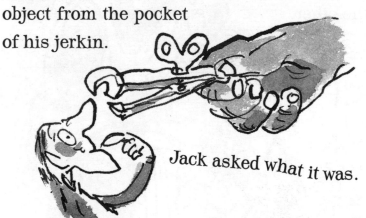

Jack asked what it was.

'It's a toenail clipper,' the giant informed him. 'First of its kind. What do you think?'

'Fascinating,' said Jack. 'But...'

'But?' repeated the giant warily. Critics!

'Well, what's the point of a giant toenail clipper?' Jack asked.

'There's quite a lot of point if you have giant toenails,' answered the giant, wiggling his extremely large toes, which stuck out the end of his giant open-toed sandals.

'Mind if I have a look at it?'

'Be my guest,' said the giant.

Inspecting the giant toenail clipper, Jack became thoughtful. He looked up at the broomstick climbing all the way to the sky, on which the multitude of ripe new cans clanked in the breeze.

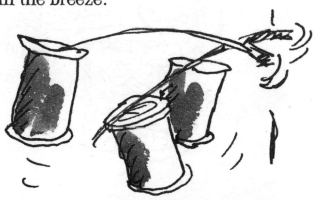

'Hmm,' he said.

'What?' said the giant.

'Would you be so kind as to pick one of those tins for me please?' Jack asked.

The giant plucked a can of beans from the teetering broomstick and handed it over. Jack attached the giant toenail clipper to the edge of the can and turned the handle.

And guess what.

The lid lifted, easy as winking.

'That's clever,' said the giant.

'It is,' said Jack.

'Giant,' said he,

'stay as long as you like!'

And stay the giant did, and his toenail clipper became the world's first can-opener. This was extremely timely, there being such a lot of unopened cans in the vicinity. Fortunately, both Jack and the giant discovered a liking for baked beans. Liking? Nay, a love of them. They couldn't get enough of them. They stuffed themselves silly at breakfast and brunch, at lunch and linner, at dinner and dupper and supper.

They were good times, if a tad breezy.

And so they might have remained had Jack's nagging old bag of a mother not found her way down the broomstick and spoilt everything.

But that's another story.

One you're not going

to find in this book.

Sorry!

FROM a JACK TO a KiNG

This story takes place in the tiny tucked-away kingdom of Raggedass. Like most kingdoms, Raggedass had a king and queen, and in the course of three decades Queen Twess of Raggedass had given birth to four children.

The eldest was Prince Effluvium, the second eldest was Prince Vomitus, and the third eldest was Princess Nettlerash. Only the youngest, the last born, did not bear a royal-sounding name. He was called Jack.

Prince Jack was called Jack for a very good reason. The very good reason was that his parents couldn't be bothered to think of anything more grand for him. Why? Because they were ashamed of him. Ashamed because, unlike them, unlike his brothers and sister, he was very short. I mean really short. No one that short, they decided at first sight of him, could possibly command the grovelling respect of the common people.

At the age of seven the top of Prince Jack's head was on a level with his father's knee. By the age of ten it just about reached his father's cod-piece. Three years later it ran parallel with his father's nipples, and there it stayed.

On his fourteenth birthday, still only nipple high, Prince Jack received an unusual present from his parents. A wooden hut. The hut had been specially built for him on the very periphery of the kingdom, between the gate and the steaming cesspool where Raggedass's waste was dumped. The birthday gift came with a royal note ordering him to keep away from the palace from this day forth because the hut was his home now. Besides, the note concluded, someone had to close the gate. The young prince, a lad of generous spirit who only ever saw good in people, felt that a great honour had been bestowed upon him.

Proudly he planted flowers round his hut, oiled the hinges of the gate, and every two days, because no one else would do it, put on a gas mask and stirred the cesspool with his rolling pin to stop a skin forming.

In contrast to Jack's humble hut, the royal palace, which stood at the top of Raggedass Hill, was a splendid sight. Quite spectacular it was, all white and gleaming, with lots of towers and turrets and cupolas and flags, and battlements patrolled by dashing sentries in dazzling armour and helmets luminous with peacock feathers. The king and queen, who lived there with the two taller princes and their daughter, had no doubt who would inherit the throne once they kicked the royal bucket. It would go to their eldest son, Effluvium.

So let us now turn to that noble prince. Heir to the throne of Raggedass and tallest of the royal bunch, Prince Effluvium loved hunting. He loved hunting because he loved killing things. He would have hunted his own people if his father hadn't thought it might make them revolt. 'They're revolting enough already,' the king often said, without one whit of shame.

So the prince had to content himself with hunting down helpless animals. It was quite good fun, especially the bit at the end where he leapt from his horse with a princely 'Ha-ha! Now I have you!' and lopped their defenceless heads off. In his time Effluvium had lopped off at least one head of every species larger than a fist in the kingdom.

The only head not
to grace the walls of
his apartments was
that of the giant boar,
which was almost
extinct. When news
came that one had been
spotted in Raggedass Forest the
prince whooped for joy, called for his
saddled horse, and rode down the hill
and into the forest with forty bodyguards,
beaters, archers and hairdressers.

Little Prince Jack watched the hunting party from the step of his hut between the cesspool and the gate. He would have cheered it on if he hadn't felt sorry for the boar. But he needn't have worried, for when the boar emerged from the forest half an hour later, far ahead of the pursuing entourage, it was quite unharmed. Prince Effluvium wasn't feeling too fit though, lying on the beast's great tusks and twitching out the last two and a quarter minutes of his tall life.

'Ho, old boar!'
cried Jack as the boar
lumbered in his general direction.

'What have we here then?'

'It was him or me,' replied the boar, who'd learnt to speak on his travels in other forests where boars were more respected.

'I see your point,' said Prince Jack. 'Both of them actually.'

The boar's step faltered. A burly prince on your snout can take it out of you rather. 'I suppose you'd better kill me and get it over with,' it sighed resignedly.

But this did not appeal to little Jack. In fact, the very idea boared him silly. 'I wouldn't dream of killing you,' he said. 'I love animals, even animals as ugly as sin, like you. Anyway,' he added philosophically as his parents' tallest son gasped his last, 'I have another brother.'

And so he had: Vomitus, new heir to the throne of Raggedass.

Now Prince Vomitus wasn't much like his slightly taller but rather late older brother. He wasn't as surly for one thing, though what he lacked in surl he made up for in girth. In other words he was fat.

Very fat.
Stupendously,
ridiculously,
out-of-all-proportion fat.
The reason Vomitus was so

huge was that he ate too much.

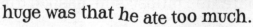

As Effluvium had lived to
hunt, Vomitus lived to eat.
Nothing in all the world was
as important or interesting to
this prince as food. He liked
to eat and eat and eat, and
when he'd finished eating
he liked to eat and eat
and eat some more.

But about a fortnight after he took over the
position of heir-to-the-throne, something
happened to make Prince Vomitus lose
weight dramatically. It started with the
horse-drawn cart that pulled up one morning
outside the hut between the cesspool and the
gate.

'Pigs' eggs!' the driver cried.
'Finest fresh pigs' eggs
for sale!'

Prince Jack came to the door. The tradesman looked down at him and smirked at his smallness. If he'd known he was in the presence of a prince he might have shown more respect, but Jack didn't look much like a prince. His clothes were ordinary, his hair was uncombed, his fingernails were bitten and dirty. He didn't even speak royally. His parents had bothered so little with him while he was growing up that he'd played with whoever he pleased – the stable lads, the royal cat skinners, the dung collector's apprentice – with the result that at fourteen he was as common as muck on a bad day.

'Since when did pigs lay eggs?' Jack said, inspecting the cartload of large pink eggs with curly little tails.

'Have you never heard of genetic engineering?' the tradesman answered. 'Now listen, Shortstuff, I'm willing to let you have this load   that's about three hundred eggs – for just forty coin of the realm. What do you say to that?'

'I say I haven't got forty coin of the realm,' said Jack. 'And even if I had, what the blithering heck would I do with three hundred pigs' eggs?'

'They boil well,' said the man. 'Five minutes from boiling point to eggcup and you never tasted nothing so rich and satisfying in your little life. Five thousand calories per yolk. Just one will keep your stomach quiet for a whole day. Two, and you'll feel that you've eaten like a prince, or even a king.'

'And if you eat three?'

'You spend the next forty-eight hours on the bog wishing you'd never been born.'

'You could try the palace,' Jack suggested, pointing it out in case he'd missed it.

'I'll do that,' said the pigman, and headed for Raggedass Hill.

Now by chance the new
heir to the throne was
looking out of a third-floor
window as the tradesman
drove up. Noticing the three
hundred large pink eggs
with curly little tails,
Prince Vomitus's
pupils dilated.

'I say!'

he bellowed out of the window.

'You! My man!

What hev you got thar?'

The eggman tugged the forelock he'd bought at the joke shop in the next kingdom. 'Oi got pigs' eggs, moi 'oighness,' he said, in that idiotic way that peasant tradesmen speak to royalty or the disgustingly rich. 'Three 'unnered on 'em, oi got.'

'Hev you, bay Jove,' said Prince Vomitus, who had speech problems of his own, but royal ones. 'Are theeeey...taysteh?'

'Lor luv yer, sorr,' said the jolly eggman. 'Tasty? Oi should say so. An' on'y two 'unncred coin o' the realm the laat.'

'Stay rate there!
Dewn't move a muscle!'

The prince unjammed his shoulders from the window and went through the loose change in his piggy bank. 'Ketch!' he said, tossing down a hundred and ninety-eight coins and two buttons.

The man tucked the loot into his shirt, tugged his new forelock once more, delivered the eggs to the kitchen, and drove back down the hill at a rate of knots, chuckling. Prince Vomitus, meanwhile, sent word to his disgruntled cook to boil the three hundred eggs to 'ebsolute parfection' and serve them in his personal dining room in forty-five minutes flat.

In forty-six minutes flat (rebellious lot, these peasants) the three hundred freshly boiled pink eggs were neatly arrayed on a pristine white cloth in the prince's dining room. Vomitus slapped his overweight lips and tucked a napkin the size of a sheet into his collar. He placed a footman on either side of him to whip the tops and tails off the shells as fast as they could so he could shove the contents down his gullet without pause and save himself from starving.

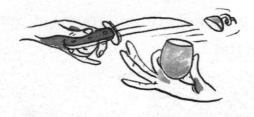

The first egg went down in a fraction of a trice. 'Yum!' cried the prince, and popped another in. 'Double yum!' cried he then, blithely reaching for a third, then a fourth, a fifth, a sixth, and so on, letting rip a right royal belch after every other one.

While the rest of the world went about its business with varying degrees of sanity, Prince Vomitus continued to shovel calorie-rich pigs' eggs down him as if there was a reward for stuffing yourself silly. There was, in a way. When Vomitus gulped down the thirty-second egg his poor abused stomach gave a great gurgle, then a great ripple, and his body unzipped all down the front, flipped inside out with a sharp *ssshlup!* and the royal innards slapped against the opposite wall, where they bubbled and steamed messily all the way down to the floor.

Vomitus of Raggedass had pigged out once too often!

During the standard period of compulsory national mourning (during which a surprising number of pigs flew over the land) King Twinge and Queen Twess tried to decide what to do. They had a problem, you see.

Raggedass law decreed that heirs to the throne must be male, which meant that their new heir should be Jack, runt of the royal litter. But they couldn't bear the thought of such a short unroyal person some day becoming ruler of their glorious kingdom, and after much deliberation and consultation with fawning advisers, the king issued a proclamation stating that the law had been changed.

Princess Nettlerash was now next in line to rule!

When they heard who had been proclaimed new heir to the throne, the people shuffled about muttering 'Shame, shame,' as peasants do if you don't oppress them enough.

But Prince Jack just shrugged. He had his little wooden hut between the cesspool and the gate. What did he want with a kingdom?

So Princess Nettlerash became heiress to the throne of Raggedass.

Now there's something you ought to know about this princess, and that something is this. Nettlerash simply could not bear dirt of any description. She didn't mind looking at dirt when it was on the ground, or when it was on her lowly subjects bowing and scraping as she swanned by in her golden coach with her royal nose in the air, but she hated – I mean *hated* – to have any of it on her. She changed her clothes every four hours, bathed twice a day in warm milk (semi-skimmed) and washed her hands after touching anything, even herself. This is far more important than you might think, so please remember it.

On a particular afternoon in the noble history of Raggedass, Nettlerash, heiress apparent, was out in her coach looking for common people to wave haughtily at with a stiff hand. The coach was going too slowly for her liking because the driver was old and frail and only doing it because he didn't have a pension to fall back on. Nettlerash constantly leant out and screamed at him but, though the old coachman did his best, the horses steadfastly refused to obey his gentle urgings.

At last the frustrated princess ordered the man to stop the coach, banished him from Raggedass for the remaining two weeks of his sad old life, and got up behind the horses herself. She whipped them soundly for their tardiness, and they, knowing better than to say neigh to royalty, shot off without further ado.

Faster and faster they went, and the faster they went the more the princess enjoyed herself, whipping them until their ears flattened against their skulls, their eyes started from their sockets, and foam appeared at the corners of their big horsy mouths.

When Prince Jack saw the coach hurtling towards him his first thought was that the horses were out of control. He stepped boldly into their path with his hand up, in that

'Stop right there !'

attitude that
runaway horses
the world over
recognise instinctively as a command to ignore. However, at the very last, Nettlerash's horses changed their minds and veered sharply, just missing Jack and his hut, which put them on an unscripted collision course with the cesspool.

Fortunately for them, the horrendous smell reached their flaring nostrils before they galloped into it and they again veered off. This second veering was so sharp that the royal driver lost her grip on the reins, left the coach at a steep angle, did a spectacular triple somersault in mid-air, and came down head first in the foul sludge.

But Nettlerash didn't drown as you

might expect.

No.
She died of disgust!

Immediately following the third state funeral in two months, the cesspool was designated a National Shrine in Memory of Beloved Princess Nettlerash, which visitors were encouraged to visit for a small fee. Some peasants paid the fee just to wee in it.

On a certain morning in June, two long, lean packages were delivered to the hut between the gate and the National Shrine in Memory of Beloved Princess Nettlerash. Inside one of the packages Prince Jack found a pair of extremely long trousers and a brace of stilts. In the other he found two ultra-thin footmen who'd been given the job of helping him into the trousers and onto the stilts.

There was also a note from his father
ordering him to put the stilts to good use and
make his parents proud of him after all.

Later that day King Twinge addressed the nation from a palace balcony. The heir to the throne, he announced with reluctance, was now Prince Jack, the only royal child left with a pulse.

'But he will *try* to be taller,' His Maj assured the people.

Mindful of his duty, and with the help of the footmen provided, Prince Jack got up on the stilts and began practising a tall person's walk. He didn't find it easy, but after a week of earnest stilting he started to get the hang of it, and in a fortnight he was quite enjoying himself. Being so tall now, taller in fact than the tallest man in the kingdom, living or dead, he had a loftier view of the world than he'd ever had before.

It was perhaps because of this that Jack began to change in certain ways.

He started brushing his hair,

cleaning his nails,

wearing better shirts,

and giving orders where previously he had asked politely if he wanted something done that he couldn't do himself.

He took to treating his future subjects as inferiors rather than equals too, which he'd certainly not done before. In fact he became increasingly like his parents and his extinct brothers and sister.

He was saved from becoming *exactly* like them by an accident. Or maybe it wasn't an accident. (Anyone who stands out from the crowd, or above it, gets an ill-wisher sooner or later.) Scumbox the royal poacher later swore under torture that the night before it happened he heard a sound like wood being sawn quietly near the prince's hut, right about where the stilts were leaning.

That fateful morn (with forecasts of storms, lightning, hurricanes and possibly snow) Jack got on his stilts, commanded his faithful underpaid footmen to pull his trousers up for him, and began stalking about, hands on hips, between the gate and the National Shrine in Memory of Beloved Princess Nettlerash.

With his nose in the air, as had become its habit, he was unprepared for the sharp lurch forward when his stilts cracked in two and dumped him in a horse trough half a stilt away.

Brought so unceremoniously down to earth (and spluttering a bit), Prince Jack lifted his dripping head just in time to see a tornado spring from between two mountains to the east and whirl towards Raggedass Hill. As he watched, the tornado reached the royal palace, felled the splendid turrets and cupolas like skittles in a bowling alley, and carried off the utmost tower containing the bedchamber of the king and queen.

'Oh dear,' said Prince Jack, wiping horse water from his troubled brow.

'I hope Mama and Papa aren't still in bed.'

But they were;
and as the tower span
round and round
in the mighty
maw of the
tornado, two nightgowned figures shot
shrieking from the window. Far below, the
adoring people watched their king and queen
hurtle towards a sheer escarpment, heard the
royal screams abruptly cease as – *Thwik!*
Thwuk! – four royal arms and four royal legs
spreadeagled into two melodramatic outlines
on the rock.

A full nine and a half seconds of wordless shock and horror followed before the wretched peasants fell at the feet of the only surviving royal personage in Raggedass, who, by an unexpected twister of fate, was now their king.

King Jack addressed his people. 'Rise,' said he. 'I've learnt a lesson here. I've learnt that one should never try to be what one is not.'*

'But you're the king,' grovelled the nearest pathetic subject.

'Aye,' Jack said. 'But a king who's not above any one of you, except the odd child. So let's be done with all this bowing and scraping and live happily together.'

* No, I don't know how the royal berk came to this conclusion either.

He was as good as his word.

Little King Jack, as he became known, never looked at another stilt. Nor did he have the royal palace rebuilt, but merely added a small extension to his hut to accommodate the royal chamber pot, hoisted a small royal flag, and hammered a small crown above the door. As king, Jack was greatly loved and respected throughout Raggedass, mainly because he didn't get on his high horse all the time. Ever, in fact, because he couldn't without stilts.

And there you have it. The story of a Jack who became a king. A warm and cosy tale which should, by rights, end something like this:

So Little King Jack lived a long and happy life.

Except it wouldn't be true.

Not quite.

He lived a short and happy one, though.

JACK and the GiANT-KiLLER
AND JACKWiTCH   978 1 40830 714 8

JACK and the BROOMSTiCK
AND FROM a JACK to a KiNG   978 1 40830 715 5

JACK-in-the-BOX?
AND TALL-TALE JACK   978 1 40830 716 2

JACK FOUR'S JACKDAWS
AND JACK of the GORGONS   978 1 40830 717 9

All priced at £4.99

The Jack stories are available from all good bookshops,
or can be ordered direct from the publisher:
Orchard Books, PO BOX 29, Douglas IM99 1BQ
Credit card orders please telephone 01624 836000
or fax 01624 837033 or visit our internet site: www.orchardbooks.co.uk
or e-mail: bookshop@enterprise.net for details.

To order please quote title, author and ISBN
and your full name and address.
Cheques and postal orders should be made payable to 'Bookpost plc.'
Postage and packing is FREE within the UK
(overseas customers should add £2.00 per book).

Prices and availability are subject to change.